The Whipple-Scrumptious JOKE BOOK

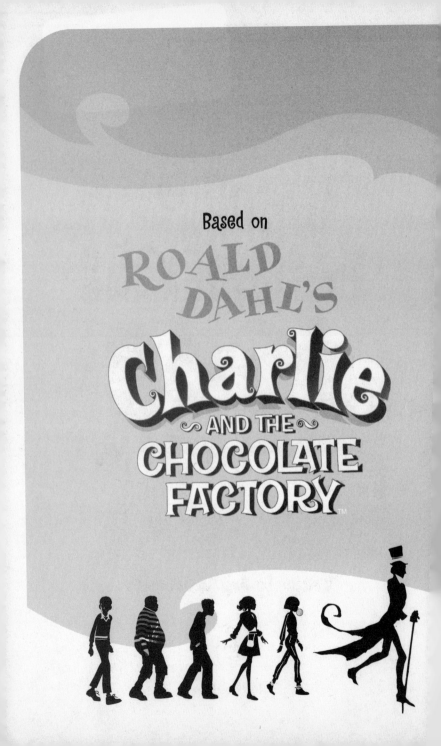

Based on

ROALD DAHL'S

Charlie

AND THE

CHOCOLATE FACTORY™

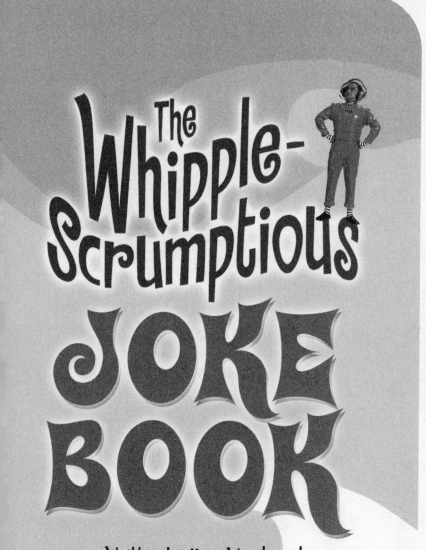

The Whipple-Scrumptious JOKE BOOK

Written by Kay Woodward

PUFFIN

PUFFIN BOOKS

Published by the Penguin Group
Penguin Young Readers Group, 345 Hudson Street, New York, New York 10014, U.S.A.
Penguin Group (Canada), 10 Alcorn Avenue, Toronto, Ontario, Canada M4V 3B2
(a division of Pearson Penguin Canada Inc.)
Penguin Books Ltd, 80 Strand, London WC2R 0RL, England
Penguin Ireland, 25 St Stephen's Green, Dublin 2, Ireland
(a division of Penguin Books Ltd)
Penguin Group (Australia), 250 Camberwell Road, Camberwell, Victoria 3124, Australia
(a division of Pearson Australia Group Pty Ltd)
Penguin Books India Pvt Ltd, 11 Community Centre, Panchsheel Park, New Delhi - 110 017, India
Penguin Group (NZ), Cnr Airborne and Rosedale Roads, Albany, Auckland 1310,
New Zealand (a division of Pearson New Zealand Ltd)
Penguin Books (South Africa) (Pty) Ltd, 24 Sturdee Avenue, Rosebank, Johannesburg 2196, South Africa

Registered Offices: Penguin Books Ltd, 80 Strand, London WC2R 0RL, England

First published in the United States of America by Puffin Books,
a division of Penguin Young Readers Group, 2005

1 3 5 7 9 10 8 6 4 2

Based on the book *Charlie and the Chocolate Factory* © Roald Dahl Nominee Ltd, 1964
Images copyright © Warner Bros. Entertainment Inc., 2005
Text copyright © Roald Dahl Nominee Ltd, 2005
All rights reserved

Written by Kay Woodward

ISBN 0-14-240389-X
Printed in the United States of America

CONTENTS

BUCKETS OF LAUGHS

Why is Charlie's house full of Buckets?

Because there are so many holes in the roof.

What dance did Mr. Bucket
do when he put tops
on toothpaste tubes?

The twist.

What does Grandma Georgina
think of her husband?

She thinks he's George-ous.

What happens when the
Bucket family eats
cabbage soup?

It gets really windy.

What's small, wooden, and
fills with water?

The Bucket family's house.

What

do you get

when you add together

the ages of Grandpa Joe,
Grandma Josephine, Grandpa George,
and Grandma Georgina?

A calculator!

VERY SILLY SWEETS

What candy is the kindest?

Care-amel.

4

What did the outlaw
say to the
lickable wallpaper?
This is a stickup!

Which detective solves
confectionary mysteries?
Sherbet Holmes.

What do you call a lollipop
that can build a bookshelf?
A handy candy.

Did you hear about the chewing gum that never loses its taste?

It's always very stylish.

Which squashy sweets
do you find
on boggy ground?
Marshmallows.

What sweets fall
from trees?
Lemon drops.

What do French people
say when they taste
a really good sweet?
"Bonbon!"

What do Oompa-Loompa
cowboys use to catch horses?
Licorice ropes.

Why did the shop owner
give away chewing gum?
It was sugar-free.

What's a janitor's
favorite
Wonka candy?
The Everlasting
Glob-mopper.

8

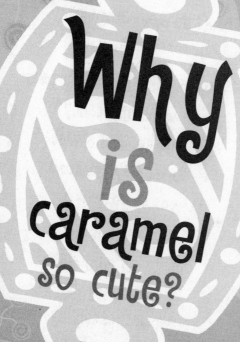

Why is caramel so cute?

It's a real sweetie.

9

What kind of candy
can you use for
cooking?
Pepper-mints.

Why didn't the teddy bear
want any candy?
Because he was
already stuffed.

What is an
ice cream's
favorite day
of the week?
Sundae.

Did you hear
about the person
who spent years testing
Everlasting Gobstoppers
for no wages?

He was a sucker.

Why did the gum cross the road?

Because it was stuck
to the chicken's foot.

Did you hear about the man who sold the world's biggest breath freshener?

He made a mint.

What is a geologist's favorite treat?

Rock candy.

Why was Jack's beanstalk so wobbly?

Because he planted jelly beans.

How do you make an elephant float?

With two scoops of ice cream and a glass of root beer!

12

KNOCK, KNOCK KNOCK JOKES

Mike Teavee: Knock, knock.

Veruca Salt: Who's there?

Mike Teavee: Augustus.

Veruca Salt: Augustus who?

Mike Teavee: Augustus a sunny month!

Grandpa Joe: Knock, knock.

Charlie: Who's there?

Grandpa Joe: Willy.

Charlie: Willy who?

Grandpa Joe: Willy invent
a new chocolate bar
today, or won't he?

Willy Wonka: Knock, knock.

Charlie: Who's there?

Willy Wonka: Goal!

Charlie: Goal who?

Willy Wonka: Goal-den Ticket!

"Knock, knock."

"Who's there?"

"Mike."

"Mike who?"

"Mike kind of chocolate!"

Violet: Knock, knock.

Charlie: Who's there?

Violet: Oswald.

Charlie: Oswald who?

Violet: Oswald my gum.

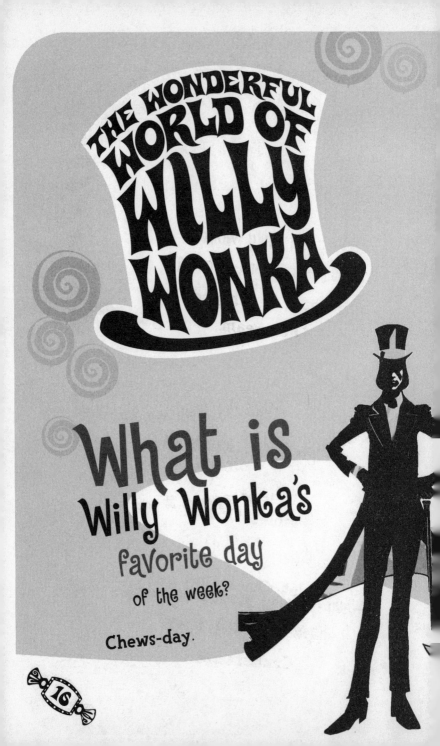

THE WONDERFUL WORLD OF WILLY WONKA

What is Willy Wonka's favorite day of the week?

Chews-day.

16

Why did Willy Wonka
punish the Oompa-Loompa?
Because he whipped
the cream.

What did Willy Wonka
do at the end
of the chocolate-bar meeting?
He wrapped it up.

When do Willy Wonka's squirrels
have their daily snack?
Crunchtime.

What is Willy Wonka's
favorite letter of the alphabet?
Mmmmmmmm...

Why do all of Willy Wonka's
ice creams grow to exactly the
same size and shape?
Because they're
ice-cream clones.

What does Willy Wonka use
to style his hair?
Chocolate mousse.

What kind of rain
falls inside
Willy Wonka's factory?
Chocolate sprinkles.

Mr. Wonka: I haven't slept for days!
Charlie: Why not?
Mr. Wonka: Because I sleep at night!

What looks like half
of a Wonka bar?
The other half!

Willy Wonka: My mother once
visited the Caribbean.

Mrs. Salt: Jamaica?

Willy Wonka: No, she went
because she wanted to!

How does Willy Wonka
fasten his shoes?

With licorice shoelaces.

Why does Willy Wonka
smile when he sleeps?

He's having
sweet dreams.

What do Willy Wonka's
chocolate cows give
after an earthquake?

Chocolate
milk shakes.

What do red squirrels
most like to eat?
Ginger nuts.

The dentist examined Willy Wonka's
teeth and said, "You've been
eating too much candy.
You're going to need a filling."
"Oh, goody!" Wonka replied.
"I'll have chocolate
filling, please!"

What are
Willy Wonka's
favorite vegetables?

Sugar snap peas.

What happened when
Willy Wonka
had a bubble perm?

His hair went
fizzy.

What do Willy Wonka's carpenters use to cut wood?

Chocolate saws.

24

What is the
most valuable candy
in the whole world?
Golden nougat.

What does
Willy Wonka celebrate
on October 31?
Marshmalloween!

How does
a nut feel when
one of Willy Wonka's
squirrels bites it?
Nut so good.

Did you hear about the storeroom at Willy Wonka's factory that was crammed full of chocolate bricks?

It was choc-a-block.

Why doesn't Mr. Wonka like ghosts?

They give him the willies.

SUGARY SWEET FAIRY TALES

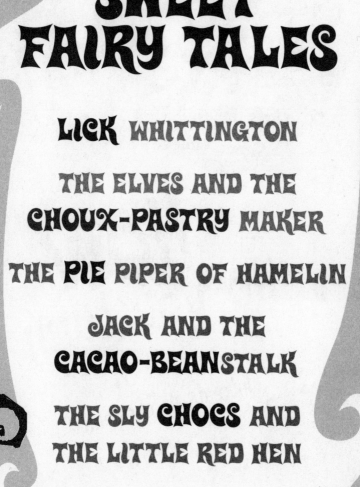

LICK WHITTINGTON

THE ELVES AND THE
CHOUX-PASTRY MAKER

THE PIE PIPER OF HAMELIN

JACK AND THE
CACAO-BEANSTALK

THE SLY CHOCS AND
THE LITTLE RED HEN

27

CHOCOLATE-TASTIC!

How do you turn light chocolate into dark chocolate?

Turn the light off.

28

What did the chocolate-covered
rooster shout every morning?

"Choc-a-doodle-do!"

What type of train takes
chocoholics on vacation?

A cocoa-motive.

Why did the psychologist turn a large bar of Wonka chocolate into a small bar of Wonka chocolate?

Because he was a shrink.

Did you hear about the warm bar of chocolate that wouldn't go out in the rain?

It was a big drip.

What do choir singers
love to eat?

Organ-ic
chocolate.

How do you make a
chocolate milk shake?

Give it a fright.

What kind of candy
do sharks like?

Shark-o-late.

Where do
Oompa-Loompa
ballet dancers practice?
At a chocolate barre.

What are stored in
chocolate factories?
Chocolate facts.

What
do you get
if you mix together
cacao beans, milk,
and sugar
for
precisely
four hours
and twelve minutes?

A sore arm.

Why do Oompa-Loompas work overtime before Easter?

They're making eggs-tra chocolate!

What did the pilot shout before the airplane with a cargo of chocolate set off?

"Chocs away!"

What do you get if you cross chocolate with a sheep?

A candy baa.

Did you hear
about the bird that fell into
the chocolate river?
It truffled its feathers.

Where does the
chocolate river spring from?
The chocolate sauce.

How do you turn chocolate into hot chocolate?
Put it in the oven.

Who performs at the chocolate circus?
Cocoa the clown.

What's the best way to keep your chocolate from melting on a hot day?
Eat it, of course!

Did you hear about the chocolate teapot?
No, me neither.

THE GOLDEN TICKET RUNNERS

What time

do the **chocolate factory** gates open?

Ten o'choc.

Which Golden Ticket
winner likes potato chips?
Veruca Salt 'n' Vinegar.

What's small and makes a
loud noise on television?
A Mike.

What does Augustus Gloop
like to do in his spare time?
Jigsaw guzzles.

How are Veruca and
sour milk alike?
They're both spoiled.

Why did Mike Teavee
feel all wobbly?
He'd been watching
too much
jelly-vision.

When Augustus Gloop
pours chocolate
into his mouth,
where does it go?
Down the glug-hole.

What did Augustus
do when he fell
in the chocolate river?
He decided to go
with the flow.

Which Golden Ticket
winner can perform tricks
in an airplane?

Augustus Gloop-the-gloop.

What happened when
Augustus Gloop got stuck
in the pipe?

A choc-wave ran
through the factory.

What happens when
Miss Beauregarde
eats too much chocolate?
She is Violetly sick.

What did Mr. Beauregarde
say when Violet turned
into a blueberry?
"By gum!"

Why did Violet Beauregarde
shrink?
She ran out of juice.

Who
is the
scariest
child in
Willy Wonka's
factory?

Violet Boo-regarde.

43

Veruca Salt:
We just flew back
from New York!

Mike Teavee:
Really?
Your arms must
be very tired.

Do Mike's parents
have a
plasma-screen
television
at home?

No, they have
a tiny Teavee.

Did you hear about Violet Beauregarde,
the champion gum chewer?

She came to a sticky end.

What happened when Augustus Gloop
fell into Willy Wonka's river?

He went for a chocolate dip.

What did
Charlie say
say when he was
sucking an
Everlasting
Gobstopper?
Nothing—it's
rude to talk
with your
mouth
full!

46

How did the cricketer
get into Willy Wonka's
chocolate factory?

With a Golden Wicket.

What do Augustus Gloop
and a bendy, fluffy stick
have in common?

They're both pipe cleaners.

What happens when
Miss Beauregarde stands
under a spotlight?

She turns ultra-Violet.

EVEN MORE KNOCK, KNOCK KNOCK JOKES

Charlie: Knock, knock.
Grandpa Joe: Who's there?
Charlie: Justin.
Grandpa Joe: Justin who?
Charlie: Justin time
for chocolate!

48

Mr. Bucket: Knock, knock.

Mrs. Bucket: Who's there?

Mr. Bucket: Candy.

Mrs. Bucket: Candy who?

Mr. Bucket: Candy Great Glass
Elevator fit through the roof...?

Charlie: Knock, knock.

Willy Wonka: Who's there?

Charlie: Wafer.

Willy Wonka: Wafer who?

Charlie: Wafer me—
you're walking
too fast!

First Oompa-Loompa: Knock, knock.

Second Oompa-Loompa: Who's there?

First Oompa-Loompa: An éclair.

Second Oompa-Loompa: An éclair who?

First Oompa-Loompa: An éclair day,
I can see Loompaland.

Augustus Gloop: Knock. knock.

Willy Wonka: Who's there?

Augustus Gloop: Ivana.

Willy Wonka: Ivana who?

Augustus Gloop:
Ivana Luminous Lolly!

WONKA TREATS

What does a turkey do when it sees a bar of Wonka's Whipple-Scrumptious Fudgemallow Delight?

It gobbles.

51

What do you get
if you cross Luminous Lollies
with Wriggle Sweets?
A pain in the tummy.

What runs
but never walks?
Mr Wonka's chocolate waterfall.

Did you hear about the boy who
slurped too much Wonka
lickable wallpaper?
He was very pasty.

What is the best thing to put in a Willy Wonka chocolate bar?

Your teeth!

What's chewy, tasty, and makes your bangs stand on end?

Willy Wonka's Hair Toffee!

Did you hear about
the chocolate river that
ran through the
chocolate factory?
It turned into a tunnel.

What is better than a bar of
Wonka Whipple-Scrumptious
Fudgemallow Delight?
TWO bars of Wonka
Whipple-Scrumptious
Fudgemallow Delight!

Why did the bar of
Wonka's Nutty Crunch Surprise
miss the party?
Because it was
choco-late!

What is

Willy Wonka's walking stick made of?

Cane sugar.

AWFULLY SWEET JOKES

What kind of bars won't keep someone in jail?

Chocolate bars.

56

What do you call a
doctors' practice where
everyone eats sweets?

Sugary.

Who plays sweet songs
on the radio?

A disc chocky.

Why did the boy
dip his cross old
auntie in sugar?

He wanted to
sweeten her up.

What do you call
a well-behaved child
who steps in molasses?

Gooey-Two-Shoes.

How do you make
a Swiss roll?

Push him down a hill.

Did you hear about
the doughnut
that wore a really
sweet jacket?
It was sugar-coated.

Did you hear the one about
the singing shiny paper?
He was a wrapper.

What runs but never gets out of breath?

The chocolate river.

66

Why did the cream scream?
It didn't like being whipped.

What did the dentist say
when his patient told a joke
about his sweet tooth?
"That's rotten."

What sort of book
tells the reader how to
drink very hot chocolate?
A re-sippy book.

THOSE

LOOPY

OOMPA-
LOOMPAS

What do you need to know to teach an Oompa-Loompa tricks?

More than the Oompa-Loompa.

What do
Oompa-Loompas
shout when they hit
peanut brittle with a
sledgehammer?

"Smashing!"

What do you call
an Oompa-Loompa
with edible marshmallow
pillows in his ears?

Anything you like—
he can't
hear you.

63

What do you get if you cross
one of Mr. Wonka's helpers
with an Australian bear?

Koala-Loompa.

Willy Wonka: My favorite
Oompa-Loompa has
a blocked nose.

Charlie: How does he smell?

Willy Wonka: Terrible!

What great sporting event
takes place at Willy Wonka's
chocolate factory every four years?

The Oompa-lympics.

Why are Oompa-Loompas
so short?

Because their heads are
so close to their feet.

Where does the Oompa-Loompa
teacher write her assignments?

On a choc-board.

Why do Oompa-Loompas
paint their feet brown?
So they can hide upside down
in the chocolate.

What do you call a talk show host
for Oompa-Loompas?
Oompa Winfrey.

Why did the
Oompa-Loompa
cross the road?
It was the
chicken's day off.

THE CHOCOLATIEST BOOKSHELF

ADDICTED TO CHOCOLATE by Y. Stop

CHILLY CHOCOLATE DESSERT by I. Screem

CHOCOLATE EATING ON THE RISE by Ellie Vator

Expensive Chocolate by Milly N. Dollars

How to Tell When You've Eaten Too Much Chocolate by R.U. Full